The Werewolf Family

Story by Jack Gantos   Art by Nicole Rubel

HOUGHTON MIFFLIN COMPANY BOSTON 1980

Library of Congress Cataloging in Publication Data

Gantos, Jack.
    The Werewolf family.

    SUMMARY: At a family reunion held when the moon is
full, the Werewolf family astounds its relatives with
bizarre behavior.
    [1.   Werewolves – Fiction.   2. Family – Fiction]
I.   Rubel, Nicole.   II.   Title.
PZ7.G15334We   [E]   80-14083
ISBN 0-395-28760-X

One evening the Werewolf family was getting
ready to go to their family reunion.

"I wish we could stay home," said Mrs.
Werewolf.

"Me too," said Mr. Werewolf. "Family
parties are so boring."

"And I feel awfully strange tonight,"
said young Harry Werewolf.

"Me too," said Mary Werewolf. "Maybe
we shouldn't go out at all."

"Now children," said Mrs. Werewolf.
"There is no need to worry. It's probably
only because of a slight change
in the weather."

"There's a full moon tonight," announced Mr. Werewolf as he looked out the window. He had become very hairy. Even the dog had changed.

Suddenly the Werewolf family had an
uncontrollable urge. Without another word
they ran outside and howled at the moon.

"HOWLLL!"

"HOWLLL!"

"HOWLLL!"

When the Werewolf family arrived at the family reunion, Uncle Boris greeted them at the door.

"What side of the family are you related to?" he asked.

"Not mine," sneered Aunt Charlotte. "My side of the family doesn't have such big teeth."

"Nor mine!" declared Uncle Igo. "My family doesn't have claws or red eyes."

The Werewolf family began to foam at the mouth. "GROWLLL!" they replied. They pushed everyone down and burst into the house.

"Now run along and have fun with your cousins," Mrs. Werewolf said to Harry and Mary.

"HOWLLL! GROWLLL!" cried the Werewolf children.

"They make friends so easily," remarked Mrs. Werewolf.

"We must try to be friendly," said Mr. Werewolf to Mrs. Werewolf. "Remember, we're all family."

They gave the little children some gifts. The packages were filled with snakes and furry spiders. The children screamed at the top of their lungs.

"I just adore the sound of howling," said Mrs. Werewolf.

"Me too," agreed Mr. Werewolf. "It's so cheerful."

Uncle Igo decided to show home movies. "Would anyone like a snack before show time?" he asked.

Mrs. Werewolf crawled across the floor and bit him on the ankle.

"Maybe she doesn't like home movies," said Aunt Charlotte.

Then Aunt Charlotte announced that dinner was served.

"GROWLLL!" cried the Werewolf family.

"We have a lovely soufflé," said Aunt Charlotte.

"I prefer live cat," snapped Mr. Werewolf.

After dinner the Werewolf children felt restless. "Let's bob for apples," they suggested.

"O.K.," replied their cousins.

"You first!" yelled Harry and Mary.

"Let's play Little Red Riding Hood," said Mary as she smacked her lips.

"I'll be the wolf," said Harry as he smiled sweetly at cousin Cissy.

"I understand this house has been in the family for centuries," said Mrs. Werewolf.

"Would you like a tour?" asked Aunt Charlotte.

"Yes," replied Mrs. Werewolf. "Let's start with the basement first."

Then they all trooped downstairs.

"What a lovely recreation room,"
exclaimed Mrs. Werewolf.

"Every home should have one,"
said Mr. Werewolf.

"Just whose side of the family are
they on anyway?" asked Uncle Boris.

"They don't look like anyone I know,"
said Uncle Igo.

"Well, they certainly aren't mine,"
gasped Aunt Charlotte as she fainted.

"Come along children," said Mrs. Werewolf when the family reunion was over.

"Hurry up," said Mr. Werewolf. "The moon is already sinking."

The Werewolf family returned home and went to sleep.

The next day Mrs. Werewolf said,
"I had a great time last night."
"So did we," said Harry and Mary.
"Yes," remarked Mr. Werewolf. "We
should get the family together more often."